P9-BZP-205

This edition published by Parragon in 2012
Parragon
Queen Street House
4 Queen Street
Bath BA1 1HE, UK
www.parragon.com

Copyright © Parragon Books Ltd 2011

All rights reserved. No part of this publication may be reproduced, stored in
a retrieval system or transmitted, in any form or by any means, electronic, mechanical,
photocopying, recording or otherwise, without the prior permission of the copyright holder.

ISBN 978-1-4454-7793-0

Printed in China

Cinderella

Retold by
Kath Jewitt
Illustrated by
Dubravka Kolanovic

PaRragon

Bath · New York · Singapore · Hong Kong · Cologne · Delhi
Melbourne · Amsterdam · Johannesburg · Auckland · Shenzhen

Once upon a time, there was a kind, sweet girl named Cinderella. Her mother died when she was very young, and her father married again.

His new wife and her two daughters, Anastasia and Drusilla, were mean. They treated Cinderella like a servant.

One morning, there was a knock at the door. Cinderella opened it to find a stylish footman. He handed her a gold envelope.

"The palace is holding a ball for the Prince's birthday tonight," he announced. "Every girl in the kingdom is invited."

You are invited to the Prince's birthday ball.

"This isn't for YOU!" cried Anastasia, snatching the invitation.

"But the footman said that every girl is invited," protested Cinderella's father.

"Of course she may go," said Cinderella's stepmother slyly, "as long as she has finished all her chores … "

But no matter how hard Cinderella worked, her list of jobs just kept growing. Her stepsisters and stepmother made sure of that.

"Iron my dress!"

"Brush my hair!"

"Polish my nails!"

"Fetch my necklace!"

"Oh dear!" giggled the stepsisters, when the coach arrived to take them to the palace. "Aren't you ready yet?" And they flounced out, laughing unkindly.

Poor Cinderella sat by the fireside.

"I wish I could wear a pretty dress and meet the prince!" she sighed.

Suddenly, the room was filled with sparkling light as a fairy appeared.

"Dry your eyes, Cinderella," said the fairy. "I am your fairy godmother—and we have work to do!"

"Go to the garden and fetch me the biggest pumpkin you can find," her fairy godmother said.

SWOOSH!

With a wave of her wand, Cinderella's Fairy Godmother transformed the pumpkin into a beautiful coach.

Next, the fairy godmother searched the
courtyard and rounded up four white mice and a rat.

SWOOSH!

Four gleaming white horses and a
stylish coachman appeared.

"Now for you," said the fairy godmother.

SWOOSH!

Cinderella's plain dress was
transformed into waves of soft silk,
and on her feet were two glass slippers.

"Now remember," said her fairy
godmother, "my magic won't last.
At midnight, on the final stroke of
twelve, everything you see before
you will disappear."

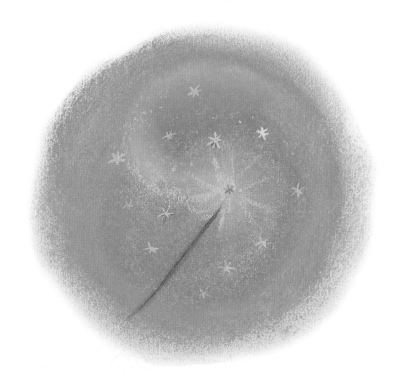

When Cinderella entered the ballroom, the guests couldn't take their eyes off her—and neither could the prince. He rushed over and asked her to dance.

Anastasia and Drusilla watched grumpily from the side.

Suddenly, the palace clock began to strike. BONG! BONG! Cinderella remembered the warning. The magic was about to end!

"I'm sorry!" she cried. "I have to go …"

The prince chased after her, but
he was too late. All that remained
was Cinderella's glass slipper.

The next day, the prince set out to find the beautiful girl from the ball.

"Every girl in the land must try the slipper," he said.

Girl after girl tried to squeeze her foot into the tiny slipper, but with no success. Finally, the prince arrived at Cinderella's house.

Anastasia and Drusilla fought but they could not force their big feet into the dainty slipper.

"Let Cinderella try," said her father bravely.

The prince slipped the slipper onto Cinderella's foot.

"It fits!" he cried happily. "My search is over! Will you marry me?"

Cinderella agreed at once.

"But she didn't even go to the ball!" shrieked her furious stepmother.

Suddenly, the fairy godmother appeared. She transformed Cinderella's dress into the beautiful ball gown once again. There could be no mistake—Cinderella was the one!

The prince and Cinderella got
married and lived

happily ever after

in the palace.

Meanwhile, Anastasia and Drusilla
had to polish their own shoes and iron
their own dresses—and that made them
grumpier than ever!

The End